Charlie is
My Darling

For Sorcha, Méabh, Cillian,
Liam and Aoife – M.D.

For Mali – S.L.

ORCHARD BOOKS

338 Euston Road, London NW1 3BH

Orchard Books Australia

Level 17/207 Kent Street, Sydney, NSW 2000

First published in 2008 by Orchard Books
First published in paperback in 2009

Text © Malachy Doyle 2008
Illustrations © Stephen Lambert 2008

A CIP catalogue record for this book is available
from the British Library.

ISBN 978 1 84616 797 3

10 9 8 7 6 5 4 3 2 1

Printed in China

Orchard Books is a division of Hachette Children's Books,
an Hachette Livre UK company.
www.hachettelivre.co.uk

Charlie is My Darling

Malachy Doyle • Stephen Lambert

ORCHARD BOOKS

There was a dog in the
window and he barked.

There was a dog in the window
and he wagged his fluffy tail,
and he gave me such a look
with his big brown eyes,
that I knocked on the door
and said, "Hello," to Ellen Adams.
"There's a dog in your window
and I think he wants to play."

She said, "Charlie is my darling,
and he always wants to run.
But the only time I'm out is when
I'm shopping, with my stick."

Well, Charlie looked at me
with his big brown eyes,
and I knew what to say.
I said, "I'll take him
to the park."

The old woman smiled and said, "You're very, very kind.
But you'd better hold him tight
or he'll be home with Ellen Adams.
Yes, you'd better hold him tight
or he'll be gone."

So, I put him on a lead
and I took him to the park.

He trotted right beside me –
he's a very clever dog.

So, I let him off the lead –
I was sure that he'd be good . . .

. . . but he pinned back his ears

and he ran!

He ran so fast that I couldn't even catch him.

He chased around the lake and he leapt into the water.

Then he shook himself all over someone trying to read a paper.

"Wait, Charlie, wait!" I said,

and reached out to grab him,

but he saw a little rabbit
on the grass,

and he was gone.

He was racing,

he was chasing,

he was, *"Bark! Bark! Bark!"*

He was
crashing
through
the trees,

and he was flashing up the hill.

I clambered to the top
and I looked all around
but I couldn't see him anywhere . . .

I couldn't see him anywhere.

"Oh, come back, Charlie,
won't you come back, Charlie,
please, please, please."

Oh, what am I going to do?

Oh, what am I going to say?

Oh, what am I going to tell
Ellen Adams?

But then I heard a barky noise
from somewhere round about.
A funny sort of barky noise.
A Charlie sort of barky noise.

I ran

and ran

and ran . . .

. . . and it was him,
in the window
of Ellen Adams'
house!

"You're a very naughty dog," I said.
"You're not to run away!"

But he gave me
such a lick with his
long wet tongue . . .

and he gave me such a look
with his big brown eyes . . .

that I knew what he was saying,
as he wagged his fluffy tail . . .

"I'm just a dog
who likes to run,

who likes to play,

who likes to paddle,

likes to breathe fresh air,
who likes to race back home
to Ellen Adams."

So, I knew what to say.
"I'll come and see
you every day,
but you're not to
run away again –
I'll always bring
you home."

And I said to Ellen Adams,
"He's a dog who likes to run,
who likes to play,
who likes to paddle,
likes to climb up hills,
who likes to breathe fresh air,
                    like me!"

So, now I've two new friends –
Charlie Dog and Ellen Adams.

One is young and fast and yappy,
one is old and slow and happy,
and I'm glad.

I'm very glad.